THE RED PRINCE

Charlie Roscoe & Tom Clohosy Cole

templar publishing

Once, there was an island kingdom called Avala.

The king and queen were much loved by the people and their son,
the prince, was friends with every child on the island.

One day the prince's parents set off on a grand tour of the mainland and
left the young prince in charge. As they set sail, dark clouds rolled over
the island and snow began to fall. A storm was setting in.

The Avalans shut their doors and lit their fires. Almost no one saw the black ships that sailed silently into the harbour . . .

. . . or the strangers who leapt ashore,

snuck through the streets,

seized the city,

and captured the prince.

They took him far away and hid him in a fortress in the heart of the island.

Locked in the dark for days, the prince lost all hope.

But then, one night, he saw his chance.

The prince ran . . .

. . . and ran.

The alarm rang out over Avala . . .

. . . and soon the island was crawling with strangers,
all searching for the little red prince.

He stumbled through the snow, until he saw
the flickering light of a fire.

A young girl sat beside the flames.
"You have to get to the city," she told him.
"Your friends are waiting for you."
"But how will I get there?" asked the prince.
"The strangers are everywhere."
"Don't worry," she said. "You'll find help in
the most unexpected places."

As the prince made his way across the island . . .

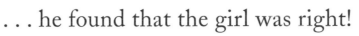

. . . he found that the girl was right!

The Avalans did everything they could to
confuse and confound the strangers . . .

. . . and the red prince was able to sneak all the
way to the city gates.

He could hear a great commotion from behind the walls,
but saw no way past the guards . . .

. . . when suddenly they were distracted,

and he slipped inside.

There, he saw something
he couldn't believe.

All of Avala were dressed as red princes! The city was filled with ruby red and rang with laughter and music.

The prince danced through the streets for hours, invisible
in a sea of brilliant colour.

Until he left the safety of the crowd.

The strangers chased him down,

but the prince was no longer afraid . . .

. . . for he knew that he was not alone.

The strangers scrabbled to their boats, rowed to their
ship, and sailed away from the island of Avala.

Never to return.